This book belongs to:

_____

It's Going to Be Another Good Day!

by
April Matula

little pink press™

Illustrations by April Matula

Published by Little Pink Press, P.O. Box 847, Beacon, NY 12508

ISBN-13: 978-1-7329494-8-5

Good night, sleep tight.
Tomorrow is going to be
another good day.

Now try to make poo-poo.

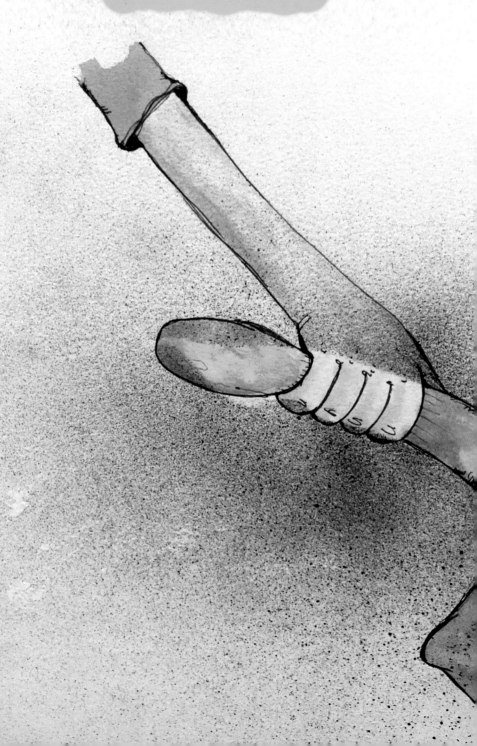

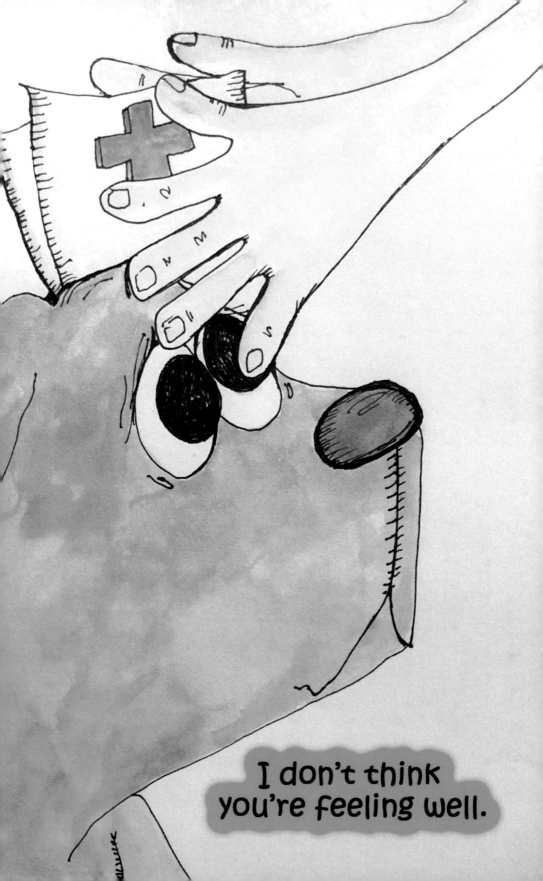

Yup, just what I thought...

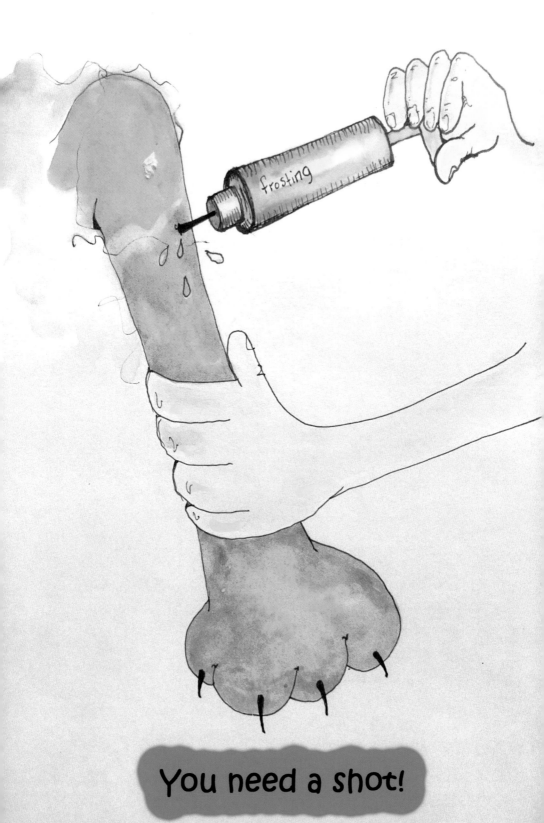

Oh, they're not laughing at you.
They're just jealous.

I really don't know how you get
yourself so dirty. Let's give you
a shower before dinner.

Let's go watch a movie
and have something to eat.

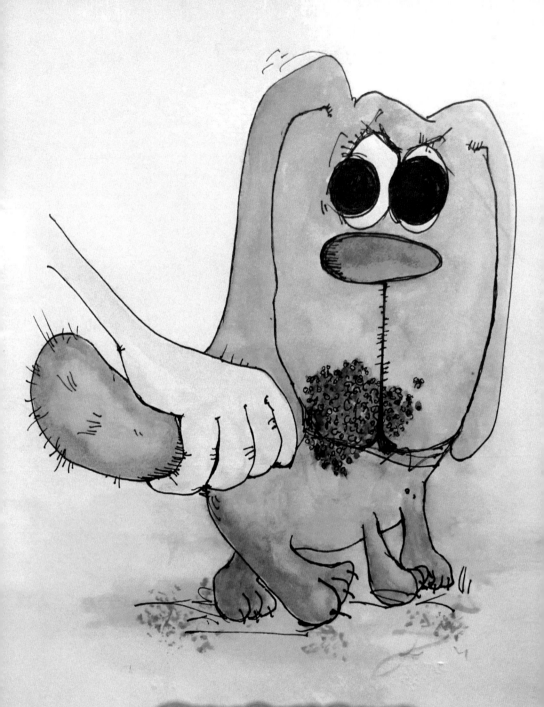

Come back here!
It's time for bed.

Now go to sleep.
Sweet dreams.

Tomorrow, we're going to have another good day!

Other books by April Matula:

It Happened Again

Lucky Larry

Oh, Lola!

Tushy Tanner

Made in the USA
Columbia, SC
27 October 2020

23576744R00018